ESPLANADE

ESPLANADE

By

JOHN M DICKSON III

DEDICATION

To Josephine LoCocco Glynn and Walter Glynn Jr, two extraordinary people who are living exemplary lives, whose template I use to live my own.

DEDICATION

To one of my oldest friends, Gerry Pedersen, may I live all my days with the exuberance and zeal with which you live one of your own.

TABLE OF CONTENTS

A Night of a Thousand Darknesses

Some are fearful of the night

and the cloak worn by demons

There are those who brandish a sword

While far more run from them

Does not that which manifests so

Not conjured with that of ourselves

What we'd rather not dredge

But leave benignly in our wells.

For, can a black cat ever strike a fret?

Can it ever cross our path

If we do not be the one,

who allows it to escape its bag

And what of those whom we believe practice voodoo

leaving upon us some sort of gris gris

Unless we forgive them a chance

can they impact you or me

Is it not merely our innate fears

that are already in place

That cause us to cower

indeed, to cover our face

For unless we do not stand tall

if we do not show our weaknesses

I believe we will not ever know

a night of a thousand darknesses

Epiphany's Son

It's been a long road and

lost time on the road away from home

Leaving my spirit and feet with

callouses from life's stones

It mattered not to me you see

as I went along

For whenever I was beaten down

I arose then with a song

Born and raised in New Orleans

quite near Esplanade Avenue

Where I learned lessons

Long since past overdue

I spent my time as a young man

down the streets of the Quarter

Where things went down in alleys

that nowhere would be like any other

There were times down there

I drank from such a cup

That even when I opened my shattered eyes

I found I could not look up

I dragged and stumbled myself back

to thumb my nose at all those

Who had taken advantage of my repose

But found when I righted myself

and gazed into the sun

I heard a gentle voice saying

Welcome you back, Epiphany's son

On Solid Ground

It's late one Saturday evening

way out back by Founder's Pond

The whippoorwills are getting ready for night

Singing their last day's song

The trout is making his last dinner pass

just there by the slough

And the barn owl startled turns his head asking

Just there now does go 'Whooo?'

Squirrels are gathering acorns

blackbird squawks his last

While I settle by my fire

Stirring my hot stew pot's repast

 I settle in with my whiskey

that I drink from my tin cup

And raising my eyes to the stars

I see as I then look up

Not the kind of time for everyone

not everybody's kind of night

but after a lifetime of uptown scheming

This suits me just right

So, if you'd like a place full of quiet

With nothing but solitude around

Come on out and see what it's like

having your feet on solid ground

Sweet February

Februarys finally arrived

Now that cold January's bid goodbye

And with it something

Not often seen in the by and by

A near foot of snow fell late

in old New Orleans

Sixty years before the likes

that which we had last seen

Mine and a generation before

in disbelief of any such

Kept in our subtropics

Usually so green and so lush

But for a couple of days

we bid adieu to the sun

As the turning of winter's leaf

that day had begun

Snowflakes filled the sky

leaving the obvious riddle

How the snowfall could create

a pristine landscape of such a stipple

Children young and old

gathered together in the streets

Amazed at what the sky showered

at that winter retreat

Welcome sweet February

we've awaited you so

May there be time enough

'til we see the next snow

THE ARCHER'S BOW

Some stare starry-eyed up at the moon

Others wish upon a rainbow

all trying to find answers waiting

For those who wish to know

Need you a magic carpet

to take and find if on a ride

A rainbow shines the same way

when seen from the other side

And does one have to board a rocket ship

To take off for the moon

to find if we will one day

Visit again soon

These are the dreamers

I count myself among

Those whom gaze up to the sky

saying let us go and learn

Rather than just sit and wonder why

For now, I am here to play for those whom perhaps

Have not found cosmic songs sung

Telling them the moon is but

a stepping stone on our way up another wrung

So, leave your earthly thoughts behind

And let the rainbow be your archer's bow

Catapulting you to a world

'til now you'd never know

The Old Jazzman

You can find him down on the Esplanade and Bourbon

The same place tonight

As he has always been

Up the street there's a bar with the name Port of Call

He sees the young men come

and slip inside those dark walls

That once there wished they'd not

given in

But the pull of painted ladies

is too much to resist

Once they have seductive hands

holding you in their grip

Yeah, he's the Old Jazzman

in a derby and a suit

He stands and pipes out New Orleans music

In such a humble pursuit

In a way that most who stop to listen

Call nothing short of magic

He's been offered other better

more comfortable Quarter paying gigs

But he always says

"Well, thank you kind sir, but I'll be staying here

'Cos 'em young boys who come 'round

Don't know what they should and shouldn't fear

Or what to do with what they found"

"In case they find they made a mistake

Know in my coronet case laying there

Is also a thirty-eight"

"The incident won't last as long as

did their little escapade"

"I'm just here to show them

the mistake that they just made"

So, the Old Jazzman keeps an eye out

No sheet music needs his eye

But he's here for those who need to get on to get by

The Vanquishing of Lucifer

In New Orleans the streetcar

rumbles down St. Charles Avenue

All the way until it makes its way

'Til Carrollton comes in view

That's where I was born and baptized

Long before I learned

I didn't belong and realized

I didn't care about it as such

That was not the crowd one

I could rely on in a clutch

So, my boys and l went out

and did what we could to change the world

While the silver spoons did nothing more

they wait for their trust fund to turn

Creating nothing other than in their spoiled heads

Would do nothing more than feather their beds

Give me a mate anytime anywhere

Who dusts himself off from a fight

The kind you want to lean on

When it's been that kind of night

So come with me warrior poet

And let us vanquish the Lucifer's waiting hem

And between the two of us

fatally fight and defeat him

Saving all others what would have otherwise been their end

WHENEVER THE TIME COMES

I feel undeservedly that ever so

Someone in pain is calling me

for I am not one whom you would

have remembered in the day's come and go

But I am afraid I'm to do something

For someone whom I don't yet know

I am no talented physician

I don't know how to stitch a wound

But I cower as I fear I'll be

called upon to do just that soon

When the Lord told Moses

he had a journey he had to undertake

He said "But Lord, the loaves and fishes

Were a meal of which I didn't partake"

The Lord told him "Worry that not my son

For a lifetime is but a day

and it being already noon

Best be on your way"

So, take up the quest he did indeed

Assuming the yolk he found himself bound beneath

The Lord assuring him lest evil befall him

He would bare his sword from its sheath

I feel too something that's expected

Something I must do

with the understanding

I will be alone whenever the time comes to.

WHERE IT NEVER RAINS

I went for a long autumn walk

on a well-known distant shore

And even in the short time there

saw things I'd not known before

I thought of things that were on my mind

things I don't understand

Such as how a river can crash against rocks

turning them into sand

How they say a cloud usually light as

can become heavy before it rains

And when the rain evaporates

it happens all over again

How a heart can say it shall break

if a love should ever go denied

Such as a rose without water

Will most surely die

And people who swear an oath

to be forever right and true

Only to have in difficult times

To abandon you

So, I invite you come and walk with me

on the shore where it never rains

And where I will always be with you that

You're not left alone again

Him

I had a thought for you

it seems a moment or so

But now to reflect on it

Seems so long ago

I sit by my fire and

I see my young man here

I could not be happier

than you have him near

ANGLES IN THE GRAVEYARD

There are no curves in a graveyard

Save the street marker's boulder stones

So, one doesn't get lost

And suddenly feel alone

When in fact in a cemetery

Please do make no mistake

You walk among the bones

Who've no mind to escape

And then of the carriage

Our escort to where we'll rest our take

A place where there is no time

No slowing or is haste

So, choose your steps wisely

Do not cross your right foot over your left

For if you hadn't to try to in life

You wouldn't be here yet

Second Line

Hey brother, where you going

on this old railroad line.

I said I got a message

of the passing of an old friend of mine.

He said I heard you were going

all the way down to New Orleans.

I see you got 'Ms Paula' packed by

there by your ripped blue jeans.

Good for them, though they don't know

Coming home, one of her boys.

Gonna strum the Quarter

bringing them a new joy.

As I'm sure you remember,

keep it in the back of your mind.

The next second line you see,

be it not you unless but it be mine

Down here in New Orleans, we live the life

We celebrate it even when we give up the fight

Some think you get bit one go round

But we don't think that's right

Yeah, we all are given

one ticket down in time

But down here in New Orleans

We got you a second line

So The Cypress Says

The fire emanating that I now strike

Illuminates a candle I light at night

Crystallizing through magical wax and stone

that which before I had not yet known

I was raised in with the Esplanade's view

Heard of some but known only by a few

Regarded in stories

Of old New Orleans lore

Told me by the elders to the young ones

Who'd not heard it before

The sun passed the moon

to yield him the night

In celebration to their delight

The mystery that hangs

as the moss no duress

Leaving what it is that forever

So the cypress says

A Big Window

I wish I had a big window

and a giant telescope

To bring the stars closer in my sight

And with them the shine of hope

I wish I had a big window

To see who was coming by

and let them know then

If comes a sunny or rainy sky

I wish I had a big window

through that which I'd otherwise not see

And also know to prepare a table

when you come to see me

I wish I had a big window

that which I could easily see through

And like a two-way mirror you could

see how much I love you

Night Wine

How can one thing be two things

Take a word to which one

But else yet it can be

Another there to some

Which is why we may express ourselves

With undeniable expression of the face best

Better than that ever said from the vest

Demonstrate love from some men

What they believe a reverence

While in others thought of it as

Perceived as nothing but indifference

Such may also be thought true

of what may be drink

To some the grain relieves

While past other lips may give pause to think

And what then of the grape

Which gives thought from the vine

Giving the philologist during the day

A difference when night wine

In My Studio

There's a place I go to each day

more so than at night

I go there retiringly

to step out of the light

The matches that I strike up there

emit a soft glow.

Helps to illuminate better

that which I don't yet know.

I listen to soothing music,

some pieces I do compose.

But the mellow strains of others

I'm sure, I favor over those.

Along my lengthy bookcases

are my collected instruments.

Guitars, mandolin, Irish flute, and piano

which bring me contentment.

On the walls hang more and my art collection,

some in storage like a museum rolled.

They waiting for their section

and when they may be told.

In a corner stands my easel

where I test my art as I would.

Picasso said learn as an artist would the rules,

breaking them as you could.

Finally, at my desk, my quill and parchment

that takes my mind where it will go.

All of this I do quite out of sight,

up in my studio.

SAPPHIRE SALT

Things in life are not always what they seem.

Something seen one way by one man;

Looks entirely different to another

because simply put, it can.

Sugar, for one, is always at the ready

And is sweet, it always seems.

But there is another, though not from a cane

But mined from a seam.

The rare mineral silvinite,

in Semnan Province, in northern Iran

is found like nowhere else.

Imagine if you can

That which some find what seems exotic.

An aphrodisiac of sorts, which some may seek out

To what which they may resort

Undeniably what it can do

Some find it looks like cobalt

To others of a different taste

They prefer it as Sapphire Salt

Company

Sometimes when you cut yourself

You'll know just whom you need

Someone other than yourself

Whom can bind the wound that bleeds

We all have our choices

Not always the most of prudent roads

But hopefully one where you also find a Samaritan who goes

Mistakes are always regrettable

But the only way down where we grow

So, I bid you travel finding

Some of that which you don't know

Along the way due be diligent

Escaping today to tomorrow then

assisting in this great adventure

For you the company of a good woman

Flambeaux

Listen if you would please

Hear a revelry all its own

Jazz pours from New Orleans clubs

Bouncing from damp cobblestones

They say to top off your drink

As it seems that it may rain

Once you find your goblet empty

Do fill it once again

Sometime during the day streamers and confetti will surely fall

But in the City That Care Forgot

They will mean nothing at all

Strut you as you may young man

As you swagger down Bourbon Street

Kissing an unknown painted girl

Today no need to be discreet

Dance now you to the funk lurking

Around any found dark square

And if she still be with you

Best be vigilant and aware

For a rendezvous can be had

Just so long as you know

How hot on a February night

Can burn the flambeaux

TRANSPORT TO FANTASY

Bring the ethereal to cobblestone streets

Roll floats that seem to come from the sky

Catch a trinket from a rider good

If perhaps you can catch his eye

Hang the trees with a kaleidoscope

In beads of every known color

A sight you'll see nowhere else

As it is like no other

And take up from the pavement

The currency of the day

Cash in aluminum doubloons

With goodwill in no other way

Roll you Carnival royalty

Come guests all to the Mardi Gras

Find yourself a transport to fantasy

From wherever it is you are

LESSAIZ LES BON TEMPS ROULE

It's Mardi Gras Day in New Orleans

Have you any idea what that means

On today when care's in suspense

There is no consequence

And with that you can consecrate

Anything that you may create

Things go on here that you've never seen

You simply must come and make the scene

The skies are always blue

Even the sun shines if rain comes through

As Zulu floats on by

The coconuts do begin to fly

Rex comes from high above

Singing 'If Ever I Cease To Love'

Flying the purple, green, and gold

Surrender and let the colors take hold

The black girls come strutting their stuff

While bands play beyond enough

"Pro Bono Publico"

Unlike anywhere else you could go

Come to Mardi Gras and have a good time

And liven your weary mind

While you surely will hear them say

Welcome 'Lessaiz les bon temps roule'

THE LORD OF TIME

I pay him all due homage

for from him there is no escape

But remember he heals all wounds

Of that there's no mistake

But be mindful he has a certain cadence

That no matter what tack you take

You cannot hurry or slow him

but it's he who regulates

And he has his seasons

and an allotment there for each

And if you listen and heed his words

He has lessons to teach

So welcome him some afternoon

or a gentle evening

For before you may know it

the Lord of Time will soon be leaving

Your Man

I may have some endeavour

Something that must need me somewhere

One thing you should realize

And always be aware

No matter where life takes me

and what I may have to do

Know this if you know nothing else

I will be here for you

It could be some frigid mountaintop

Of some obscure hidden sea

Nothing could long make do

with that you must without me

It may seem superficial

a grand but shallow sacrifice

But to live my life without you

simply never would suffice

So for now let us come together

that we may well join hands

You will always be my woman

and I shall be your man

FERRIS WHEEL

It's quite large and at times

can be rather scary

It goes round and round

For both you and me

Meaning, sometimes you may be on top

Others somewhat low

But that's what it's like

I'm sure by now you know

But never to worry

because whatever goes round

Always given enough time

will come back down

What is it you may wonder

what is it I so speak

That has shallow short valleys

and ethereal peaks

 Do I mention a Ferris wheel

can you hear a Scottish fife

Or is the turning I speak of

would perhaps be life?

Better Men

Love is a song I sing to you

sometimes incredibly red

Then on some days

something quite else instead

Say it, you thought the line

that it would be blue

that's not me and certainly

not ever be it you

I'm the one grounded

while you take to the sky and fly

I want sometimes to follow you

but am told I can't and I ask why

Then said because you are only man

she is, however, a mystery

And if you know it not

Yes both you, my friend, and me

So, let us a cappella sing

your waiting song to see

Believe when she joins in

better men you and me

COMING HOME

I've been gone too long

Went to find that which

I already knew

Looking for answers to questions

always there in you

I'm tired of these travels

My shoes like I

are long passed worn out

I can no longer hear

anything this side of a shout

I'm going back

to everything that I've come to miss

To do anything less

I would be remiss

I need to go back

to what I know I own

Please be waiting for me

Because I'm coming home

WEATHERVANE

I peer out my window and look to the sky

and find myself asking when and again why

Will the sun shine or will it rain

and come tomorrow will I have to ask once again

But rather than hold a finger to the wind again

I need only look to my weathervane

He tells me from whence the wind comes and its force

Whether I should douse the lights or should strike a torch

There's a rattle now on my windowpanes

Seems the coming now of the rains

I blame not the wind minder

for he knows not of the rain

But he spins 'round nonetheless

to apologize again

"Rest easy, friend", I say to him

We are all tied down safe and secure

Sleep you well when the wind dies again

Tomorrow waits you weathervane

How Deep Your Valley

It's been said life's a roller coaster

filled with ups and downs

I'm from the country where we

At times have silence as our only sound

we have mountains and valleys

What most people miss is you've got to be on or down in one

Before the other you can see

I sat once in a mountain meadow

whereupon an eagle came to rest

Said he "Be troubled not, my son,

I am here to make you your best"

I asked "Why me, mighty bird

I am merely a simple man

Or tell me, hadn't you heard?"

Said he, "I have indeed

Which is why I have flown

to lift you from the valley

That had taken you as its own"

And with that he took me up

and upon his powerful talon

Brought back the confidence

with which I had begun

So yes, you can see a hollow from a meadow

Just know no matter how deep your valley

There's always something yet below

STEPHEN AND MARTIN

One night slowly walking

with Stephen and Martin

After a night of one-on-one,

The place became 4141

I had long before then

Bought the store again

Never looking back

To what I before had lacked

Walking with Stephen and Martin

Looking out from them within

Knowing then and there

I had been done in

They two are gone now

But I still walk with them somehow

And she whom also walked that night

Is still here and that's alright

HERMES

He is not Rex nor is he Zulu

Comus is gone, Momus is too

Imperial as there is old Proteus

He, too, I'm afraid

has abandoned us

Pegasus took wing

But there is still Thoth

Which should be of some comfort to each we both

But there it seems will always be

Fleet footed Hermes for all to see

So come out on this Friday night

And see he whom travels the worlds

Of darkness and light

The Woods in Winter

Have you ever been sometime

in a place where you can clearly see

That a difference can be made

by people like you and me

Where you can see a wrong being made

that you can make right

Perhaps in the darkness

where you can bring light

A man in a park

abused by wretched neglect

Who's waiting for you

and your help he'll accept

Maybe a soul treading helplessly

in a torrid sea of sin

To have you reacquaint him

with his redemption within

Come with me please

for we've work to do Hinterland

To bring springtime color

to the woods in winter

A Deep Sea

I once heard of a young man

who put himself through college

Working the oilfields of the Gulf of Mexico

living on the edge

He thought himself better

than others who would one day thwart

But they'd seen his kind coming way before the start

He got into a card game

thinking he couldn't be beat

Little did he know

what he was about to meet

I know you've by now guessed it

he lost it all

He worked all that week

To cash nothing when they came to call

He never gambled like that again

not out there anytime soon

And never until he had read the room

I know he no longer is so foolish

to dive into a deep sea

For know if you not already

That boy was me

LOVE A GOOD WOMAN

There will always be yesterday

And we know so because we live today

But wonder regret about tomorrow can we ever say

Therefore, I bid you live well

and be it for today

Learning from what was

if for no other reason

Then, simply as a child may say

Because

Because tomorrow I may do that which

Today did not accomplish

maybe then love will call

At least that is my wish

And what might be yours

I'm curious to ask

is there something unattended to

Perhaps an undone task

I will though not solicited

offer this advice

Find and love a good woman

For that believe me when I tell you

there can be no price

Hickory Ridge

I was lost for so very long

bustling around town

Taking comfort in the arms

of whatever woman came around

One day I decided I needed a change

So having had enough of it

I went ahead, packed a bag

and I up and split

I went to a place you will not know

not Alabama, Arkansas, or Delaware

But I took to a Hickory Ridge

of where you'd be unaware

I looked inside to see

what it is I may need

Looking for guidance

I thought I should heed

And I realized it's not about

how to others you feel

Or to someone's sensibilities

you may appeal

That's only what's of import

be it only unto you

Once accepted by oneself

one only need be true

THE ONE

I went walking one morning

after a gig in the Quarter

Just a little bit past three

Sat down in Jackson Square far

To find what had been passed to me

It being a ten times three

A good night by any measure

For the likes of me

Just as I counted the bills

I heard just then I what I've known myself

When a man cries his heart to spill

I asked, "What need you friend?"

Said he "Father, you know it,

you once needed it too"

"Yes, I have my Friend sat where you do"

With that I gave him what I had gotten

from the music had played

And oddly enough

I saw him the very next day

Polished and profound

And I said, "Look at you

lost but now found!"

He said, "No never, but know this because of your kindness

will you never again play to an empty room in such duress"

I asked, "Who are you friend?"

Said He, "You have called Me Friend so,

lest you not stare,

I am the One who's friend around your neck

Hangs once again there"

SOLITARY OCEAN MINION

Sometimes I feel as though

I attempt to swim through sand

Can you imagine ignored by lifeguards

Can you might understand

To feel so utterly alone

Like walking down a mirrored corridor

With no one but the Cowardly Lion

With his innate horror

I feel that at times myself

Hiking through a red canyon

Be it no more than an abandoned Solitary Ocean minion

WHALE

I am something of a denizen deep

I cannot breathe but brethren can

So much so though unlikely

Making more akin to man

The unfettered who come searching for me

Believe I surface to put on a show

Little know they only

that I may breathe and go

If you please encounter me

simply let me be free

Is that all any of us can wish for

Yes, indeed, you and me

You know of me though

I may never have met your sight

Allow me my weaknesses

And I'll give you my might

What am I may you ask

Am I sunshine or a gale

What may I be what you thought

Or simply a man or a whale

Pay It Heed

A man of a good woman

Wakes from a heavy sleep

Unable to a promise

That he failed to keep

And what does he find let he be alone

A feast set on his table of stone

He relishes in such and though

he has had his fill

Finds himself empty still

Come to me my woman

Got you are all I need

And whatever your word

I will pay it heed

THE NIGHT FLYER

I look always for midnight skies

I hope to see them soon

And upon a good witch's air

I will glide on and swoon

Long past forgotten mists

Which clouded what I saw

I look for a weeping willow branch

Where I may rest my claw

Yes, I have flown far and wide

You have always been the limb

Looking for the truth where it lies

Over my flight or within

For I have always soared through gloriously higher

Knowing in you rests me

For I am The Night flyer

Being Love

Oh, what a ship she is

Searching for following seas

To drink of the wine longer rested

There upon the lees

As the best bread baked is that which

Has had time its yeast to bloom

Such when in the coming

its aroma fills a room

To shuck the autumn corn

from October's last embrace

Has along the farmer's river

sugar cane takes its place

Indeed, as has been said,

a time for most of God's world

He sends from above

That is, of course, that which knows no season

As we all know, being love

WHERE SKIES ARE BLUE

Where go you now woman

Please it be your benefit

For to pay me of any further mind

Would not of me be fit

For as you see and know well

I am a simple man of ragged pants

Whom you above all else

Know too well and understand

My hands are roughly hewn

And well for the work I've done long

Always to an unrelenting drum

But never to a sweet song

That I have always looked past the horizon

Hoping what I add up at day's end

Will make an adequate sum

I find some do and others don't

But you never asked me why

And because I sleep little at night

I can hear you cry

I don't always have an answer

If you stay with me I will stay with you

And we will one day go

where the skies are blue

Cottage With Me

Why does the summer sunlight hoard

the laughter we know at noon

Or why the winter solstice steals music

all by we needed too soon

Why do children stay young

for so little time at all

While the rest of us try to recapture

The youth that we try to recall

Why did I not know just 'til then

how to tie a mainsail to the mast

Or have anyone ever told me

that the wind does never last

That coin well-earned and then saved

and feverishly in those kept banks

Would one day have set sail

without so much a seafaring thanks

Aye, but I worry not for

the voyage has sun and gale

And so long as we are of good timber

we will always fearlessly sail

And after all our exotic travels

come time to finally thank the moor

Will you cottage with me

for I am in no need of more

The Struggling Gardens

The moon is confused as it hangs benignly

And regrettably now it seems knows not

If the night breeze now gently blowing

will soon become a piercing knot

I tie down what is usually loose

in a way we have come to be fairly known

And lock ourselves near hearth and fire

Behind good timber and sturdy stone

On genuflected knees for the outside where therein does
quietly lie

the struggling gardens

We all these years lovingly have grown

The winds they now rise up

and indeed with an impertinence

Like some French Quarter whore

Indeed they're quite what I have seen since

As thrashing you with a conjured fury

As with some assigned name

But when the rains end and the tides retreat

The ending is the same

WHITE VOICE, BLACK NIGHT

It was a pitch-black winter night

They said snow would be here soon

And sure, enough when I looked up

I saw flakes across the moon

I dropped to my knees there along the drifts that soon gathered

As if by some generation unfamiliar

Had for the first time really mattered

Living in the mountains ever

I shared what I could either my forest friends

Which, unfamiliar in their tongues, asked if that was some sort of end

I assure them it was not

That the owl be about his lot

And encouraged the beaver to continue

To tie his earthen knot

They gathered 'round to ask in unison

"Master, how is it that you know?"

I said "Merely look above you and meet Jupiter

While Venus is shining low"

Upon seeing they found themselves believing

But I said "Care not what you see

only what you may hear

for my love calls to you

She the white voice heard

Somewhere In the black night here

Epiphany's Baptism

Once met a man who regrettably

had never left his home or been anywhere

And the world as a cause of it

was all he was unaware

He took his comfort and his penance

In an Esplanade bar down in New Orleans

Where younger and more foolish thought he had found his scene

But a worldly woman had taken

a lonely night therein

And saw him out of his element

but found more than that in him

Thought with no more than a dram

She could relieve his discontent

and set about to do so

Such was her intent

As he spoke she could obviously see what there could be

What separated them was nothing short of

the widest of known seas

She said "Look, sugar, you're clearly

 in way over your head

What say we get out of here

and go to my place instead?"

Away they went into the wintery night

Where she showed him the world through a new prism

A rebirth of some sort

Perhaps Epiphany's baptism

Newly minted and reborn

with the new eyes of a child

Enough on a rough street one night

To pause a bit for awhile

Saturday's Sentinel

Have you ever made promises

and if so, did they last?

Were there any carelessly stepped on toes?

Was there any cracked glass?

And of course, the uncomfortable truths

Which you took as your vows

Have you wondered why they couldn't be kept

Too hard to keep somehow

And what then of the children

while you were off chasing skirts

Too much easier to go clubbing

to think to make it work

And what of the Saturday sentinel

where you're asked to speak your mind

Only find when confessioning

you can't always find the lines

That's why we're given a lifetime

to see what it is we may do

Only hoping when done sinning

We may still restitute

So, my friend, do choose wisely

for the pattern catches only so much

Lost chances at redemption

so do think of it quite such

Old Smoke Road

There's a story I first heard

when I was but a boy

My father took me to tell a story

And away from my toys

He told me "Son, always be careful

And always please be aware

for no matter even when it rains

There's still fire out there

It's waiting for you everywhere

to have its way with you

And if you trip to close to its flames

It surely will burn you"

I had heard of a young man

not at all unlike me

Why had he decided to cling to what turned out to be a
burning tree?

She had lured him in

and convinced him to take a bite

Turned out to be a bitter taste

that would ruin his life

Such was the destruction

And his young soul became instantly old

That now they call the abandoned place that smoulders

Forgotten Old Smoke Road

Light Up the Night

I wished to be an actor once

to appear on the screen and stage

But my visceral fear of it alone

Kept me from being all the rage

I honed my craft in song as well

and took up some stringed instruments

to accompany my song of voice

If but to none other my contentment

So I became somewhat the Stage Manager

as read in Wilder's Our Town

Who though knowing all parts by rote

Was never seen in the round

But I was heard one day singing a capella

While tidying the actors' scripts

and had a director visiting

that day in the pit

To witness early thereon

Incredulous of my voice in it

I demurred and said meekly

"Sir I would be flattered

but I suffer of the fright"

He said "Nonsense, young man,

sing in my play's rendition and find

How much loved you will be

When you lay on in your lines

And what cut will be your sight"

So take to the stage I did

And never thought in the footlights

That my dreams would be realized

And I would light up the night

THE WRITER'S RIVER

It comes and at times can be said

It hardly at times barely flows

Such can like one's musings

We've all had days such as those

And at other times the parchment overflows its banks

Those are the days to live for

For which we give our thanks

At times somewhat like love

We search for and ponder it

But it seems sometimes to find us

When we may least be fit

The tide will come early one morning

All to carry and deliver

what's been floating for some time

On the writer's river

CALL TO THE CABBIE

I once shared a cab ride

down in old London town

with a woman I knew not

but of some kind renown

I said "You are donned all in black

can you kindly tell me here in spring

Why might that be

do truth tell me bring"

She said ever so softly

"Why, John, you need not be

questioning me at last

Because you well know

I am your quiet past

I trembled in my seat

and asked her in replete

"If it is so is any future for me said she, yes at the next street

But there are three others

Intersecting

Be now so discreet

and of you so effecting"

75

One being what could have been

the second what will be

It remains yet of some sin

be it perhaps your scene"

Just then we rolled to the curb

in climbed amid beautiful music

and I asked "Kindly, whom maybe you?"

Said she "Your future, have you not heard?"

She "Your past was left at the last stop

Will you continue down

this sorry broken road or improve your lot?"

THE ROOM OF SCENT AND LIGHT

I find a soothing, and a gentling

somewhere in the stark darkness

In it too feel a gentle gathering

We may or may not confess

And we do so with all hope

In a line or two

I cannot help but search

Will you please come too

Come, come and with me

For I can make all wrongs to you right

Believe and come with me

To the room of scent and light

A Pale of Ale

The war as we knew it was still raging

the next day to register

For the draft to leave the house and mother

And all brothers and sisters

By while out that night it came

as we were on the town

Telling guns had been silenced

they would offer no further sound

Then came Hanoi had fallen

the suspension of the draft

My friend and I looked at each other

Wondering if the report heard gaffed

But no, the war was over

Peace would now prevail

We suspended plans to call it a night

And had another pale of ale

You Come Too

Throw open the windows

and make wide the doors

For down there in the street

there's music and so much more

Bring a refreshing autumn breeze

Strike in the hearth a fire

that the church sparrows gather 'round

As they cue up their choir

Oh, the life yet to be lived

I look so forward to be with you

bring forth all my children

making sure that you come too

An Instrument

I have some guitars

and they have many strings

Within them do lay songs

That I have yet to sing

I also have another instrument

It seems a corner grand piano

Waiting patiently to offer

Songs I do not yet quite know

I also have hanging around

once brought an Irish flute

The music comparatively offering

Sweet low hanging fruit

And finally a burnished player

a beautiful sunburst mandolin

The music of which is you

come to me from within

Of all these what can one say

there is such contentment

So play along with me, love

Simply choose an instrument

BECAUSE OF YOU

From the mountains of Jamaica

come Dunn's River Falls

None had I seen anything quite as beautiful at all

My parents visited once they them

When they showed me their still photographs

I was as no more than ten

They told me perhaps were I lucky

I may see them too

Little did they know before I did

I'd be forty-two

All the more was I fascinated

by what I found there in such foreign lands

All the more to it

More than I could understand

I now know of London, Paris

Glasgow, and Murano

The magic that of course is Rome

Only because of you

do all this world

I can now call home

Midnight Blooming Rose

She needs very little from the rain

to note that would be me

No attention from sunlight

to be all whom she can be

You will only find if ever tried

if ever thought you could

For she grows and blossoms only

in the shade of the wood

How is it you ask does she

need next to nothing from the sun

nor from the likes of me

why a mystery surely begin

Why because of a certain way about her

I'll try to explain that you may see

that which in a different time

will surely come to be

For you'll find her in no garden

as garland for a picket fence

But if you know where to look

you may find her hence

For you must go into the woods

for you see she is one rare of those

If you do ever find her you'll not forget

The midnight blooming rose

Always On Go Forward

I have known you all my life

and all of what has been yours

You have bound my battle wounds

And I yours from before

You have always defended me

as I have done for you

We have asked all of each other

To hear "Anything for you too"

We have fought for each other's wife and queen

In ways in which none of the three

could ever say they've seen

or could ever be

We have spent many saddled days together

In lands not of our own

Only to find we'd been knighted

when we fin'lly returned home

Let us both live long and well

and against each's enemy cross swords

That we may both press on with our grandchildren

And always on go forward

Snow Leopard

If ever found I am in the mountains

Higher than most you can ever trek

Where I roam the jagged heights of Nepal

Where ambition's bones are kept

You will never hear me roar

But may well hear my growl

But I will not engage you

Unless you threaten me somehow

I am an avid climber

Unlike one you've ever seen

I straddle the crest of the peak and sun

When not in a ravine

When needed I can bound

beyond my six-foot creep

In needed I may well jump

To trounce from o'er twenty-five feet

Again, not one you've ever seen

and even far fewer ever heard

I am right in your plain sight

I am the magical snow leopard

In The Garden of Rain and Sand

I take shelter in my thoughts

in whatever way I find

Meditating on what will come

from the corners of my mind

Will I write a cogent play

that will touch people's lives

Where evil once again is vanquished

And the hero then survives

Will I compose a symphony heard

in auditoria throughout the land

Will I turn like me the common man

in a way he understands

Is in my quill the prose

that will grace some fine parchment

That those who find themselves wanting

May find some contentment

Will I abide in a fine castle

one of the finest in the land

For if not this simple man will live

In the garden of rain and sand

Stone and Sling

There was once a young shepherd boy

He was the son David of the Hebrew King Saul

Whom when Israel was threatened by Goliath

had not the courage to engage him at all

It fell to David to defend his people

Against the aggressor Philistine

It was believed to be a fool's errand

To engage in such a thing

But with his sheer bravery and his faith in his Lord

A battle ensued the likes of which

had not been seen before

The champions squared off to fight

And what then occurred a miraculous thing

The young shepherd defeated the towering giant

With but his stone and sling

Beneath a Blackbird Moon

It's quite late now tonight

indeed, early in the morning when

After looking skyward for an hour

Lies nowhere something that I was viewing until then

There may at times be changes

in the disposition or there in the heart

But when a star I named for you

disappears and shines apart

I find myself a wondering

Will the next glance will pierce my hope

I look along in the darkness

Through the lens of my scope

Indeed, as the blackbird does

In spring and too autumn

Feeling the need between dusk and midnight

Head to the warmer south of France to another place to be known then

I find a need for change wondering

if I've done all I can for you

If I've kept the promises of what

I always said I'd do

I suppose I will know sometime

Please sometime coming soon

No doubt to be revealed

Beneath a blackbird moon

Tomorrow Offers

Morning came early today

Last night had just gone bye

I said good evening to the moon

As the sun was on the rise

Clouds passed by a waving

Saying some rain may come soon

Not no unlike the song heard last

A gentle night breeze tune

Today is quietly unfolding

A gentle calming way

The kind of hours I search for

Within each and every day

I wish you well today my friend

May it be all you hope for

Better than yesterday

As tomorrow offers more

FREE THE SONG

I heard a song early today

that I had not before

It only had verses a few

thus, I found I wanted more

Its melody was sweet

and the lyric straight and true

And the more I listened there

it reminded me of you

It sang of walks along the lake

and of hikes within cool woods

The dream-like state it brought me to

Held more for me than thought it could

I returned home and took to my strings

To recreate its sound

but for all my chords a changing

What I searched for could not be found

It haunted me throughout the night

so engaged was in my head

It sang me to sleep

when I laid down my head

I woke the following morning

and headed downstairs for breakfast

And managed to find a bit of the song

Or somewhat like it more or less

I pondered it a bit more

but it came complete when you came to dine

Seeing you I can only imagine

did free the song from my mind

THE NEXT BEND

It's noon today Friday in February

And I find myself in, of all places

In love

With all its faces

Some of them are red

And the occasional blue

But none the matter

So long as there is you

The sun today is shining

Sometimes it does in fact rain

But then the sun comes out again

Is that not what it is life

At times a bit cloudy

Or clear

What was once in the distance

Soon enough is near

Ah, but love is itself a story

A beginning but that true no end

For what else it offers

Is around the next bend

That Autumn Evening

Late one September evening

in the throes of early fall

I went walking ln the woods for

no real reason at all

The river birch was peeling

as were the town church's bells

Alerting the townsfolk of a service

presently to be held

But I was having my own quiet

a reclamation there of sorts

So to the message ringing

I gave no retort

The thrush cocked his head at me

as the brown squirrels chuckled and played

By the stream a racoon soaked the feast

that he would have that day

It seemed the world caught in that moment

was all that it should be

I wished to hide there in my woods

For fear beyond what I could see

Is there not a place ethereal

As it did that autumn evening

If this were such Elysian Fields

I would never think of leaving

FOOTSTEPS DOWN THE HALL

I sit up writing quite often late at night

With hard times and soft candlelight

Though it seems I am alone

I at times sense something quite unknown

As if something or someone

that or whom has come to pay a visit

I can see nothing in the darkest

So I find myself wondering just what is it

I wonder what may soon step from the shadows

Knowing until such may happen

And reveal itself that I may never know

By I see nothing which yields me comfort

I call out to the emptiness

But am answered with no retort

Leaving indescribable distress

I turn back to my writer's journal

To scribe yet another line

But cannot forgo the foreboding

Lurking yet still in my mind

I feel a presence ever still

Wondering whom is keeping me company

Somewhere part of an animated mural

Someone whom in which I cannot see

I finally retire my pen to pedestal

As I have written my all

In time enough to recognize

the footsteps down the hall

Stroll Down Esplanade

I had some of my first adventures

Down along this storied lane

Smashing beer bottles in the schoolyard

One of many mistakes I made

Down on Esplanade

There's a bar down closer to the river

Where I lived and died several times

But where I fell in love but once

At least so in my mind

But times have a way of opening one's eyes

And as the years file past

One learns to recognize lies

On the lighter side of thirty

I married in the church of the very schoolyard

I found so smashing as a youth

My tuxedo was that day of jacquard

Shaw found such inequity

That youth is wasted on the young

No sweeter or truer song I can name

Has ever yet been composed and sung

I remember well those times

Now with my wife of forty year

and all the previous ones given me

That I do so hold so ever dear

So, return with me for a while

I walk I hope you with me made

Joining me one afternoon

For a stroll down the Esplanade

WRITTEN IN ITS STEAD

I walk quietly past where she sleeps

Not willing to disturb the dreams

she walks among

That host songs I've written as a background

Left to be by others sung

There are softly pleading guitars

and keyboards that trip as does a stream

Over strains of melodies come tripping

Over the stones as in those dreams

Willow on the cut bank holds fast

Where the current gouges the deepest trough

Just before it does so

Leaving a strand of a beach somewhat enough

Come morning she will rise from sleep's rest

With music yet afloat in her head

Hoping among it there be one

That I had written in its stead

Forever

I bid you to stand by the door

Rain cascades, thunders then my name

I am all the more empowered

to its chagrin and shame

Water's river may cut a canyon

Through up impervious solid stone

As idled by Michelangelo

So finally, so horned

Can I do water seas do

can I fashion stone

In a way one may wonder

where could such of this world call home

Or am I relegated to parchment and then to a quill

I ever strive to write

To you forever and until

The Wicked Witch of the East

She's the only one we never saw

And is spoken of with green reverence

But it seems she met her end

As some sort of doled penance

Her penalty came so swiftly

Accompanied by a dove

By way of something unusual

To ever come from above

Known for some red and white stripes

Visible but for a moment

Leaving behind envy

And all that it foments

Who is this doomed character

Who we've known all this time the least

Well, had you ever been to Oz

She's the Wicked Witch of the East

DEMONS

It's now the middle of the night

Sometime a bit past two

Did you see him dart from the shadows

Most for me he came

and not for you

I went down from my garret

From which I saw him through

He bid me to do what I was told not

That to have you come down too

I told him "Spirit, you've no quarrel with her

Or did not in your dastard plan

When in its conception

Never once ever occur?"

Further I said "I know you not corporal

Or be you of not ether

For it matters not for I will vanquish you be either"

With that he drew his furious sword

I did to humiliate him saying

"Need you the weapon I'd a fool

For I have thoughts more powerful

than any such tool"

With that his demeanor changed

From defiant to one scared and shy

I did but blink my mind's eye

And with that I bid him die

With that I saw his soul descend

To the Underworld

Where he was to come to know his end

Will no redemption flag unfurled

The lesson forthwith being this

Fear you not when you know you're right

And you will just so dispatch with ease

Your demons lurking at night

Come to the Carnival

Two weeks ago, there was snow

But the sun's shining again

But they say that by week's end we'll need

Due shelter from the rain

Soon enough though floats will go by as doubloons fly

All for the time of year it's Mardi Gras

For no other reason than because

Bands will play both night and day

And a few remaining bugle corps

Like many ones used to see long ago

In another time before

So if you're of a mind won't you leave your cares behind

and come to the Carnival

And see what you've never seen

all too wonderful

I'll be down on the Avenue

Between Milan and Marengo

If you choose to come

I'll be there waiting as I'm sure you know

All This for You

If my cape were to catch fire

and I went down in flames

Would you still love me as

you did once and again

If the blinding snow surely came

As we had been told it would

would there be what to rely on

Ever hunting the night's wood

Were I to one day set sail

and hence become lost at sea

Would you keep a watch at night

And await the search party

I ask but for all one reason

as I would and so much more do

As I once did take such a vow

doing all this for you

The Midnight Cat

I looked out my garret window one night

and what do you fancy I see

the emerald eyes of a midnight cat

Staring ominously back at me

She sees the shaking of my hands

in fact, a downright tremor

Exposing the folly, I try to mask

behind which my deceit's terror

Something happened just in that moment

something I'd not before seen me think

The cat reversed her course

And looking at me directly

with a knowing wink

I took from that she was so watching

Ever so stealingly pacing

that I had no cause for alarm

For there no treachery I'd be facing

I took her in and fed her

and set her before my fire

As she assured me I could sleep

as long as I desired

She watches for me to this day

on call throughout the night

And guards my door far until

does come the morning light

WITHOUT YOU

I snuffed out the candle that was lighting my humble night

She stared back at me as if to say

without me you have no light

I said kindly before you judge too bright

I am the one who struck your match

And gave you your light

You'd be a locked door without me as your latch

Demurred she said I shone alone

she me what more bright

Then without you I would only be

Simply an unlit candle without light

Fishing Time

I sometimes wander down

by the pond in my woods

Where I go to think over

what I've done and what I would

At times in fall I'll even

go there and wet a line

Thinking instead I'll leave the fish be

Giving them a bit more time

Up the way there's the creek

the pond being where it flows to

sometime back to keep from breaching its bank

I had to dig myself a slough

When I make it to the city

I've got a place on the Esplanade

Where I used to live all the time

when I still plied my trade

I mostly stay out in the country now

on the north side of the lake

Where my time is my own

and the most of it I make

I'm alone most of the time

save for the occasional visitor

While I hold each and every day

that I might hear from her

I hear she's taken up though

with another man about town

So I doubt that anytime soon

That she'll be coming 'round

So I take my walk in the woods

and find today it's crossed my mind

That today may that I decide

It just may be fishing time

TIMELESS

I've been around the world

When it's 6:00 AM in New Orleans

London is having tea at 1:00 PM

somewhere on the scene

Parisians are but breaking

for a midday supper at three

Is it as strange to you

as it seems to me

Meanwhile it's still but time for wine

In Rome waiting for you and me at two

An aperitif has not yet been served in Sydney

as it would be too soon

For there across cobalt waters

It has only now struck noon

They're sleeping at 4:00 AM in Los Angeles

While in New York stockbrokers

dive in after Mass

And at 4:00 PM in Cairo

They're only halfway through their workday

And tread along in their desert

For they know no other way

The point of all this being

Nothing more than if ever less

Time is the same but different

all across the world

But you, and you alone are timeless

All Your Whys

It's said that in any given week

there are but two days beginning with the letter "T"

Those being tomorrow and today no better truth think on
what I see

True too of love and the Idea of the Y's

That I am in truth "Yours"

And the other no less important

that simply being the letter "Y"

If life were only so simple

A road with either no turns or bends

Easily misunderstanding

Just before one meets its end

The only thing I do know

is what is unknown to me

Everything else I am afraid

is but a mystery to me

But I know this irrevocably

I will pray you all my "Y's""

If when I must leave I'll know

You gave me all your whys

Will You Come There Too

If I spend my days scribing lines on a pad

Will I leave an impression of all I ever had

I'm afraid what may be the call

That what I've done means nothing at all

I have buried songs I've yet to compose

Which would only prove their worth I suppose

If they move people in some way

To make extraordinary their otherwise mundane day

If I could take a lonely woman and somehow by chance

Gladden her smile as I propose a dance

If children would seek me out

For the pocket of candy, I carry about

Teaching them it takes more than that

to become a friend

And if I could lessen the load of a weary man

To remind him not everything should take all that it can

Do I have up my sleeve such magic

Or would it be lined in the cheap felt of the tragic

If I anxiously remove my felt fedora of a hat

Would there be found a white rabbit or an ominous black cat

Where is my signpost where, "Please show me is my way home"

Where I can find my solitude

I can if you give me directions

and that you will come there too

His Magnifying Glass

My grandfather went home today

he'd been here a good while

He with the kind of humor

that would always make me smile

When I was but a lad there was much

I would learn at his knee

And though my name is Jack

it pleased him to call me Charlie

He'd try to explain about life

and how I should expect it would unfold

I took from these times fond memories

when older I would still hold

We would pour over his library of books

reading classics in the evenings

Until the time came

when I needed to be leaving

When he became older at times to better see

On his desk he kept a magnifying glass

It wasn't expensive but nonetheless

His was up to the task

When a bit older still I would visit '

it'd be just he and me

He'd ask me of my life and loves

over a shared dram of whiskey

He'd say "My son, you've got time

and as you cast about just make sure that when you do

You've tied the right line"

He never got to meet the one

I finally got to the shore

He'd have loved her I know

of that I am quite sure

Anyway, when the time came

to go about his things one time last

I passed on the jewelry and valuables asking only

"May I have his magnifying glass"

THE MURANO VASE

Take your lampworker and fashion for me

A gather of molten quartz and do shape for me

A multi-colored vessel of pure didymium

That may shield my eyes the light of my woman's dreams

One that can be cased with multiple layers of color

Such when a candle placed within it

Casts ethereal shadows like no other

Perhaps a vase laced with gold leaf

The kind found on the Steeple of St. John's church

Down in old New Orleans

I have one such a glass blower made for my love

In beautiful Murano

Have one made too for your lady too

Should you ever go

Never have I ever seen

A place so beautiful

I passed through the ornate rooms

I drank it all in as though

I'd never find my fill

I look upon my gift given me

My purple and gold brocade vase

And suddenly I'm transported into my daydream

To that incredible time and place

Surrender

I've surrendered early to the night

and given away from you

When in fact me thinks I'd much rather

have exchanged the one and two

I spend time at my easel

etching in a leaded pencil

I commit a starved time

Your portrait I work on until

Then to my parchment

committing feelings to a line two

The very kind I should have shared

Faithfully with you

I walked a bit in Macbeth's and Hamlet's shoes

Both poorly led by strayed women

I pain for them as they should have both known of you then

I pursue that which I know not of science

And the mysteries of the corporal world

Another much more cosmic

I look for the both in the music

be it humble or exotic

Other ancient and classic literature

await yet my sight

In order to assimilate myself into the verses

I read them only at night

At times I stay up quite late

Sometimes it seems well past four

Hoping I may finally find

that which I was looking for before

Thirty in twenty and four

those would be the hours I would keep

Always searching for more

But this quest weighs a heavy burden

As such where I've chosen to go and been led

So yes, when the time has come

I surrender off to bed

YOUR APPLAUSE

Pry up the fallboard of my piano

that I may see the keys

For I've a love song I've composed for you

I'd play for you if you please

It begins as love often does with little notes lightly offered

Giving way to the body of a growing work of love

That echoes from the soundboard

against the lid above

Building in its breath of emotion

Onward to a crescendo

Mimicking the thunder

Each and every one of us does know

I am alone on this stage sometimes it seems like an empty concert hall

When I return from the wings

filled with you and no one else at all

Suiting me well I played my heart out

you could have seen it on my sleeve

Resolving I would play such as I could

And that you would never leave

The curtain finally falls

as I slip behind the crease

Hearing the hall fill with your applause

That has to this day not yet ceased

A Morning Kiss

Wake me in the morning

before you take your leave

Lest I be left as water

trying desperately to cling to

A stainless-steel sieve

True I am a man alone

Never to me a second thought

Other than what you have done

and what you've always brought

So even if I sleep soundly

I am but a shallow dream away

Allow me a morning kiss

Before you be on your way

THE BONES OF BROKEN DREAMS

I set sail on my lifetime's trek

God Himself has told me go wherever it is I may please

With guaranteed following seas so

I gather the crew on the main deck

that we may chart our course

Myself the only one to instruct and account for of course

I gave my compass a spin

Hoping it would angle seaward of the wind

When the dial movement cease to be

It appeared I was off to Haiti

Leaving New Orleans from Esplanade down the river

Out to the Gulf of Mexico

A short jaunt across the southern sea

The islands would soon enough welcome me

I tack and draw my sails as I go

Gently rocking here to and fro

But as I sail what do I see

The seafoam cresting on the waves crashing the bow

Are of a difference somehow

Appear to come cresting

In quite another way to besting

I suddenly find myself being tossed

On a sea so enraged

Thinking I came with nothing that to offer

Simply there to ravage and raid

Is not that at all that what it seems

But the bones of broken dreams

My Scrolling Conductor

I sat late last night in an ominous

fearful place

marked by those in glee

I was at a piano with laughing

black and white keys

They were full of music and themselves

Contributing to my trepidation and gloom

Their demeanor however took on a more receptive visage

When you entered the room

Laugh no more did they but waited quietly

Until I began to play from my stool

Realizing I was not in fact

some kind of keyboard fool

It was not what or with what kind of finesse I played

With you as my scrolling conductor

I became a pianist that day

A Forty Year

I once visited noble Scotland

and trekked along John O'Groat's Trail

I imagined myself in the bed chamber in Inverness

Where Duncan met his fatal travail

But Shakespeare aside

a touch never taken lightly

I wished to see more of the Highlands there sprightly

I ventured to the town square

And to my astonishment to learn

There poised was an apparition

of none other than Robert Burns

I sat down next to him

But before I could even speak

Said he "I know whom you are

and why you visit this peak

Aonach Eagach juts it's jagged jaw

Giving way to verdant meadows

The likes you never saw

But that is not what draws you here

You wish more of this scene

We have the fair women

Whose emerald eyes you've never seen

"True, Master Burns, what you say is true

Perhaps you may guide the way

that I may find her through you"

"Quite your restless spirit my son

though there is nowhere like the Scottish Highlands

To find that which has always been there guy in your hands"

"In truth you'll know what to do,

For all there is you must only look behind you"

I turned around, and as God as my witness held

A maiden stood with eyes of emeralds

I struggled for words asking her

"Would you care to walk with me"

Said she, "As I've been in your's, you been in my dreams

She walks with me to this day

across more jagged mountains

And in the verdant green if possible

I love her even more now

a forty year than then

My Muse

It's quickly approaching midnight

and an instrument calls my name

But because of the music yes you conjure in me

Her strings will never sound the same

Melodic chords played well enough

were all that I did know

But because of you music is transformed

Into refined arpeggio

And with every movement comes a mood

Giving way to a bridge

whereupon a coda waits

To play a stanza once more rich

Love me, be my muse

with a symphony as your gift

That I may compose phrase

the sort a soul to lift

ALL WE NEED

Mama, I'm out on the back of our land

and there's a scent now in the air

I'm feeling what is in the wind

Is floating something we must beware

Among the seagulls heading out from our pond

On their way out to the sea

is a bright red cinder still aflame

Streaking now on its way to me

As I gaze toward the horizon

I can't believe my burning eyes

There's a red line racing toward me

Fronting a roaring damned fire

Time for us to come to terms

And to pack up and leave

Our home perhaps for one last time

I'm afraid I do believe

But wherever it we find ourselves

wherever we may go

One thing I am sure of

Having one another is all we need to know

LOST DAY FOUND

Standing on a platform

down in old New Orleans

Thought I'd trip to Chicago

to take in the music scene

Told a friend my plan and he asked me

Why not the music here

And I said "My hometown

Has somewhat beat me down" through tears

He said "Tell me 'bout it, Pal,

but I know what you're going to say

You're leaving behind a woman

Who put you in this way"

He asked "Hey, man, would you like if I came along too?"

I thanked him and told him that no, this was

something a man alone must do

We shook hands and parted company

and he wished me well

And asked me to come back only

when I didn't look like hell

I snuffed my cigarette into the ground

and boarded with a wave but without a sound

I was gone about a year, came back and looked him up

he called me what he used to, saying, "Glad you're back, Pitch"

I said "Thanks a bunch Old Cup"

See, I had been a pitcher

he being my catcher

He used to lament to one and all

having to chase my curve ball

Anyway, he asked if I was over her

Asking if the train that left that day

The one that didn't carry me

As I was going another way

He asked me if I was back on the ground

I said not only that but had since that past time

Now had what had become a lost day found

I Can Fly

At times I feel somewhat down

lost and never be found

A prisoner with no means of escape

That no matter how hard I try

often it seems my dreams just die

That the things I do are no more than mistakes

I feel I'm out of the running race

And that I've lost all face

and it's useless to keep going on

Gotta get back in the game

and more than in only name

Time to play a different song

I'm on a new stage every day

But it's always the same old play

and the audience knows how it always ends

I feel I must try something new

and I may be able to be with you

I need to do rather simply ask why

Need to tie a new tail to my kite

that I may finally take flight

'Cos with you I do believe that I can fly

Shine Alone For Me

It's said now until February

all seven Milky Way planets will align

Best seen just after the sun for the day

Has by then ceased to shine

What a site that will be to see

astronomers from around the gather to learn

Will for at least a night or two will forget

How it is this world does turn

They and amateurs alike will gather

In the dark that night

on some summit

Far above the intruding world's bright encumbering light

They will squint and try so hard to see

What they'll not witness again

In their small lifetimes be

I myself shall not bother at all

For there's another celestial body

that won't ever cross their scopes' field

For you see the eighth planet star

I make reference to

Will shine alone with me

No Hint of Regretments

Most stories have the champion

who casts aside those he vanquishes

Who has chosen to capture the maiden

quite against her wishes

And on this nobleman's cost of arms

A sword, thistle, shamrock,

And a Trinity Knot

So there be no mistake of what he is

And where he hails from not

Fierce as a man one to meet

for all he battles all as he can

And settles then with the saved

Over a wee deserved dram

She her heart keeps for him

But he a wife and those who are in need

Whom are the wards of his estate

Who await his word to heed

His pleasure is to bow to her

but with regret offer her no more

Though lest now past their youth

they thought things be as would before

But he leaves her less than content

For even though his heart wonders he retreats

Once again to his revetments

with no hint of regretments

Tonight In Paradise

Outside nothing embraces me

but the unrelenting snow

And I'm afraid I have no home

or any other else to go

That's quite alright because I've had

a warm and goodly life

Even though she was taken early from me

Oh my God, what a wife

She prepared my meals

And at night turn down my bed

Images such I could never imagine

Buried somewhere in my head

I found a seat on a wood park bench

where I thought I might lay my head

But a stranger soon approached

and said "Friend, you come with me"

I said "Sir, it's the middle of the night

And you frighten me"

He said "Worry you not My son,

for I was too was once bound to a tree"

I went with Him and He set me before his cottage fire

And He gave me food and drink

All of which gave me a bit of time

To sit and warm my worn feet

and as I did so I began to think

I asked "Friend do I know You

Or whom maybe You"

He said "Of course you do

for I too was once alone and outcast just like you"

Just then His face became transformed

And I dropped my cup and cried

and said "My Lord Jesus, You are the One

who for a wretch like me died"

"Yes", He said "I climbed that hill of gneiss

and because your wife waits for you

You will join her with Me

tonight in Paradise

WISPY DREAMS

Come my lady to my table

that I may fill your plate

And with a cup of my best wine

allow me on you to wait

Later before a midnight fire

I will read you a poetry tome

Written by the Ancients

but whose truths today still hold

Perhaps then I'll play an antigue lute

Ma de of bended burnished wood

that if I strike the strings well enough

You'll be off to sleep if you would

Finally I'll turn down the sheets

and snuff out the candlelight

And meet somewhere in wispy dreams

Sometime later tonight

The Echo of Your Name

I trekked to a corner of my land

home to a mountain and a ravine

A place I sometimes go

to meditate and not be seen

I take provisions to nourish

my body and my soul

To sustain me for a few days

where no one else can find the way

I visit a mountaintop meadow

where tulips dance and roses glow

Among them I then spy

the Dark eyed Junco

He symbolizes transition

and much needed metamorphosis

Rather transcendental we know from prophecy

I should find such a rare bird as this

And when I finally reach the summit

to the gorge's precipice's jagged frame

I find my reclamation

Heard in the echo of your name

THE WARM INVITATION

I walk out on the frozen ground

and as I listen intently all I hear

Is the crunch of the snow

That quite rarely has been left here

Odd that as the snow that falls

Leaves so little sound

If any at all one can hear

When it finally finds the ground

If fact the only whisper heard is not much

And that only be of the blanket of it

That one's footfalls cause of the snow they crush

In fact as we walk along we two

The only sound that abandons the rest here

Is the warm invitation comforting me

I hear as you breathe

Too Young to be So Old

Here we are on this winter night

in our fine home lying in a warm bed

As we drift off to our comfort's dreams

as we lay down our well coifed heads

But somewhere in the cold darkness

somewhere hidden from our sight

Are those whom shiver in the cold

trying to make it safely

through this miserable night

I have stacks of sweaters locked in a lost closet here somewhere

When better put upon a freezing back

That good people could surely wear

We take so much for granted

having more than we could need

Seeing to our petty wants

When others could our comfort heed

Please remind me Lord would You

it could well be me one day shivering in the biting cold

Where such nights have found me too young to be so old

THE WISP OF A SNOWFLAKE

It's four o'clock in the morning

and it's bitter cold outside

They tell us a deep winter cold's a coming

With a snow few of us recall in our minds

The children will find something known to but a few

a little-known playful treat

As they flail their arms and legs

Making snow angels with their feet

It will be a breath of rare air for many

Whose spirits may find a lift

as the snow falls lightly

And gathers into modest drifts

It's been five years since

we could have a snowball fight

Such that the children will laugh and squeal

As only a child might

In fact the very child in me looks out my garret window still

To see if there's been a crescent forming

Out on my window sill

Since sleep has not visited me yet

I believe I'll keep my sentry watch

To be witness to the snow's coming

and it's first downy swatch

Time me thinks to be taken away

And be a child myself for a moment's take

And when dreams do indeed come

May they float on the wisp of a snowflake

The New World

There's a sun dawning today

The horizon in my face

I can forth in good hope

To a new and better place

Much has been lost along this brutal stone choked road

But I am encouraged in that unencumbered by the load

Come along with me my friend

There's a zephyr there on the air

That we float once again upon

The world where we were once there

a new dawn indeed is shining

Let us go forth and see

What the new world can once again

Be all that it can be

FLIGHT

It was a frigid day in Washington

but there was no chance of rain

And as my President entered the rotunda

I freed the cork on my champagne

Yes, it is a new day in America

and I am flying in great hope

For again we've gained our footing

On the stage of the world's slope

Come with us one and all

For our future burns ever bright

And all are dreams have once again

Euphorically taken flight

LET FREEDOM RING

I sit in a far corner of a very small room

In a pool of tears falling but not those of some gloom

My soul is renewed, refreshed, and in a state if joy

Not since I believe I last felt

When. I was merely a boy

I was mired in the quandary

Of these last four gloomy years

When my dreams kept escaping me

Rather than ever drawing more near

But I see a light now shining

With optimism and finesse

As we emerge from the swamp

And its eerie darkness

So come with me to the mountain top

Where we may shout with no care to stop

Let us go forth and jubilantly sing

For all the world to hear and see to let freedom ring

A Breeze

There's a sun that will dawn tomorrow morning

That I already pity for it will shine on those who care not

For then again they envy me

for they have not my lot

I have two good women asleep just there down the hall

One mine of thirty-nine year

The other blossoms in a way

None other can come near

So friend, I am sorry for you

for you will never drink from the cup of wine

Brought me graciously by these two

I see in the younger her grandmother's eyes

Both share the same mischief laid

That makes the game they love

worth ever to be played

Young son finds one of such be such as these

And life's winds that will certainly come

Will be no more than a breeze

Through My Gate

There's a beautiful young woman

coming soon to see me

Filling my heart with a happiness

you can clearly see

She's no idea how lovely she most obviously is

One day a fine young man lucky enough

May have the privilege to call her his

But for now she is with me

So he will have some time to wait

Only then can she be seen

when I release her through my gate

All I Saw Was You

The Beatles whom are still with us

They being Ringo and Paul

are still making music

While Jagger and Richards

can't be kept off he road at all

These are the kind of stars

Whom have no use at all for the sky

For they being whom they are

they can't tell you why

To them songs are like stones

in a beautiful mountain stream

If you ask them how they find them

They'll tell you they pan like everyone else looking for a gem

And at times one or two

may in fact catch the sunlight and shine

I have a song I wrote one day

just not quite right for the time

It's really not very much

not what one would remember

On the radio heard wherever you may go

Not what thought if until December

Only you would recognize it

For it was written for you alone

Or so I thought as I got calls from women

Through crying kerchiefs asking

How did a man like me know

How it is for me and others like me

Where have you been and what do you see

I've walked the bad side of the tracks

Never knowing what would be

Picking out a stone to aimlessly throw

I looked up and all I saw was you

And was all I ever needed to know

Know Not About The Cloak

I put out the morrow's clothing

For today's are long since gone

I know not if winter continues to wilt

Or will there be a coming spring's song

As the snow settles on my window sill

And forms those well-known crescents

It tells me the warming days

are a bit off yet

But therein is as Shakespeare said the rub

That does await us all

What clothing will hide what we are

Is not hidden by a shawl

Go now, go out, man, and live you

In sunshine, snow or rain

And whatever it be your cloak

I will see you again

CARRY THE FREIGHT

I've been at it for some time now

Needing to go away somewhere for awhile

Someplace I can go sit in solitude, to meditate and think

Perhaps of a mind to and have an afternoon drink

But I feel I've lost my way and i'm afraid to move

It seems that suddenly I find

that I've lost my groove

The tools I once had

are no longer of any sure use

I now retire to write solely

with you alone as my muse

Am I enough to make you happy, glad, and hopefully complete

Or am just in the game to warm another's cheap seat

Tell me what I do, what I write

Will leave others cost a care

Will upon my lines find something soothing redemption there

Tell me I serve some buried purpose

That I have an audience whom awaits

Tell me if there's a load to bear

I can carry the freight

Assure when my head at night time finally meets my pillow

That since sunrise I've learned more

than I before did know

THAT WAY

I once told friends I would scour the world

To find the woman of my dreams

But privately I knew I'd find her

Smiling at me from the seams

I looked out my writer's dawning

window

Knowing was heart was breaking too

But on the horizon I saw you

All else was new and fine

I can still feel it

I shudder as I think of that day

Never before or since

Have I ever thought that way

My Road Home

It's been a long time since

But I know it all the same

At times it can be joyous

While others fraught with pain

It is never traversed well alone

And never without fear

But not seen one still knows

Friends are always near

And you, my friend are it

Always turning to the right

When nothing shows itself but darkness

You've always been the light

Shine on, brother, shine on

Never deterred by any stone

For you are and always will be

My only road home

THE PRINCE OF THE PARK

What will tomorrow bring tell me please

Because I ask myself what did I fo to task

Did I write something worthwhile said

Was it enough I ask

Who's that man on the square

He whom invites the small children there

To gather around once more

to hear his same stories again from the same where

He's known as the storyteller

Spins his yarns for hours there on end

Yes, he's known and loved by all as

The Prince of the Park

Stories true maybe or not

While holding fast to his ankle

his trusty skylark

The children do so love him

For they know that they're are allb

he will ever to him be known

For he gave up the notion of

ever having any of his own

He hasn't much but what he does

he spends on treats on those who come to see him

And all he has ever wanted

Was simply to spend his time with them

Old Stone Road

I must go away for awhile

I have a search that so calls me

Something that eludes me

That I have to find truth to see

I hope to meet friends I know not yet

Fierce men whom will fight with me

Beautiful women whom will bind my wounds

Leaving no scars for anyone to see

I hope one shall privilege me

With the honor of a child

For I've not one to my name

A little girl whom I may raise

To her mother faithful as the same

For I have this quest awaiting

And I have some to provide for

But I fear no matter what I bring

I should always have done more

My sword hangs on the wall

And my long rifle over the fireplace

Where burns the wood of my searching

Where here I keep my best face

I have promises to keep and

and a tally of those I owe

To that end I must repair once again

To my journey on my old stone road

Writer's Widow

One day last Tuesday I recall

about a week or so

I drifted off to a sleep

deeper than one could ever know

A lady came to call

but I heard not ever a knock

When I finally opened the door I found

What had been sadly locked

The cryptic note there left along read so hurtfully

"This is your lonely last song

be it all that it can be

You spend your late nights often committing to useless lines

few will ever see them

To which they would ever find the time

Can you offer anything more

than you offer what is there yet?"

I apologize I could have offered more of right than of left

And what you've have come to see

What a good woman expects to know

Not a burdened stoned over to fall

That of a writer's widow

THE RINGS OF SATURN

I steal surreptitiously at night

wearing the darkest of shroud

Nighthawks silently sing

But to my they did shout out loud

The sun's hiding where I can't see

Only told on a stream's wake

Giving a backdrop to willow trees

As their boughs gently do drink take

The moon still has

it's shadowed hollows and crested turns

Painted in the soft pastels

Of the rings of Saturn

Last Rites at Night

I walk d antiseptic nights aplenty

People there were so crying

While others there quietly dying

Among them was a mother so

And unlike me she soon to go

And she weighed upon my mind

You see me his mother, she was mine

Just then a young man passed by

He wore but black in his cassock high

With a square of white in his tunic

I felt angels fly and a hint of music

And I said "Father, my mother lies dying tonight

Bless her please in your holy sight"

He said, "My son, I will bless her to

And she will be with Christ for your faith too

He went on saying "Weep you not

for I will join you soon"

He blessed her with oil and he crossed her head

But before I could thank him

He was gone instead

See these are the known Last Rites

As administered to hose leaving us tonight

Tin Man

I know a woodsman tall and strong

But despite his well-known strength

He was possessed of an even keel

The likes of immeasurable length

He went about his woods

taming all whom from far and near

But driven by the sort of kindness no one did ever fear

He sought to protect all who sought him out

Dispatching all those whom confronted him

And did turn enemy into friend about

Whom in his heart had taken in

He believed it not of himself

But saw himself as somewhat apart

I too truly believed it myself

to be dispossessed of heart

No matter the people tried as they do

That whatever they thought they could

But in trying to convince him

they did all they thought they should

But a fine maiden one day made her way

Into the threatening wood

to try and do whatever it was

She ever thought she could

And to the displeasure of her father

to be seen by him and all her clan

She brought a heart's lost love finally

To the lonely Tin Man

January's June

It's cold outside but here a fire burns brightly

And I sit beside it for awhile

My woman brings forth soothing soup tightly

Though I find it uncomfortable

she believes it's hers to do

As if her day is not long enough

until she feeds me she feels she's not through

I tell her "You know, love,

for all the things you do for me

this is one unnecessary"

"Nonsense" says she "for this is merely a token of you see

What you have done for me and our family"

I told her no matter I believe I've

somehow fallen somewhat short

"She said come now, dearest one

all you need do is look about you"

Was her cogent retort

I did indeed look about to find

all the instruments I play as a start

Hoping one day I play well enough

To serenade more than my art

But better still as I peruse the walls

I find what lifts me when I'm low

Smiling back at me are my children and their children

The only ones I'll ever know

I care not what of their provenance

I'll take whatever I'm allowed

and when asked how what I take them

I say there's no measure

To weigh of how I am proud

After a dram by the lilting embers

I will carry myself to bed soon

And once I cast off to sleep

I shall dream of January's June

A Quiet Life

It's a cold January day today

and a chilly wind prevails

The rain that begins to fall

is more like sleet than it be hail

It softly falls to the sidewalk

and makes for icy streets

Such that the traffic that shuffles along

is reduced to a snail's creep

Those whom opt to sup do so snugly

Near a fire in the corner café.

When word comes through to advise

there'll be no more work today

So it's in the offing for the day's balance

But for another afternoon's measure

The take the day in one's own time

With all due deserved leisure

A fine idea at times don't you think

to stop and take of what one's stock

To take time seeking a certain peace

Through questions at one time locked

Time enough will come to venture home

Where another waits for you in earnest

To finally come to realize

A quiet life is in fact best

The School of Infinity

There's a regimen to be followed

quite demanding to be sure

In how of thought and action

Ways you could never ever be sure

Along the way one may make mistakes

There will be no avoiding them

so long as one learns what happens

And repeats them not again

One treks along as best one can

Meeting friend and foe alike

one be known during the day

While the other lurks at night

Important to know which is which

where one may place one's trust

Better to know the sooner than later

And that of course is a must

And if nothing else my friend

find a good woman for your journey

One whom knows more than you

and ever and much more than me

And where is this place

is it in fact where you are

Or is the vector lying before you

Preordained by your own star

no celestial body lights your way

But you still can surely see

so long as you remain a student

Of the school of infinity

PAULA'S HARP

I was up late one winter's night

trying to write a little piece

But long or short it mattered not

'cos I found no peace

So I then deferred to thought's trough to have a wee drink

But no matter I found

that I still couldn't think

I went back to my table

and gathered up my quill

But it seems no line would visit

there was nothing yet still

But that all changed with a knock at my garret door

And stepping inside was the muse

with whom I needed no more

And just as the color warming

and accenting her cheek

I found my elusive music

And the lyric I did seek

Once there I found it

so very easy to heart start

And I went on to compose

what became Paula's Harp

Shine On

Oh, what a night I'm waiting for

and what it's going to be

For the winter stars are all aligned

and they're coming to shine on me

They may be dressed quite simply

but there's only one way as a star

With moondust swirling about them

There's nothing as beautiful than they are

Necklaces and bracelets worn

an accompanying angel sings

More spectacular to see there

they outshining Saturn's rings

Mercury cannot move swiftly enough

While Venus has turned envy green

Mars' love is beaming heart red

Such that you've never seen

I may not ever visit space

I need not with my own galaxy

And if my stars were ever to shine on you

You'd wish on them to be me

The Arts

My pencil in my hand on my paper

traces what life offers

When you use the soft side it's employed

It shades that what we live for

all that to be enjoyed

But as the lead grows older

and finds it's lost its edge

And a rounded point

Is gripping hopelessly to the ledge

We find we rely on what we know now

And now we're relying on the writer's quill

To offer the net that we finally

Rely upon we give in until

And when we are safely on the ground

whom are those we find holding the net

Why they would be the poet and the artist

waiting for you there yet

Abandon not what you read

or what it is you see

For the arts have been waiting through the millennium

To make you all that you can be

A Shot on The Dock

Walking along the riverfront
on the docks in New Orleans

Looking in a bag of whiskey to find
Just what it is life means

A paddle boat goes shuffling by
as it has for two hundred year and thirteen

Some of the most majestic things
that I'm sure you've ever seen

Peaceful river wakes lap up
on understanding shores

Such forgiveness they offer
but a man invariably wants more

My bottle crashes to the wood
and my paper bag does sport a cut

It is of no use to me now
Though it is all I have but

Just then behind me it seems
an angel approaches me

The kind you might well expect to find
when the nighttime clock strikes three
Said she "So sugar, what's your fancy?"

I replied "My fine rouged lady
you are more than kind

and though I have the inclination
I haven't the coin you hope to find"

She said "Honey, I knew that just to look upon you
and I'm thinking you may be to me
As you could to be me too"

I told her how lovely I found her
and had been cruelly that very night been wronged

Said she "How appropriate that is
for I pegged you as a writer of such songs"

Further said she, "If nothing else me thinks I believe
we could both use a stiff drink made

Agreeing, we went to leave the waterfront
and made our way to Esplanade

To a bar where some of my first memories
Were made quite some time ago

A place I'd not visited
since having been badly love damaged so

But before we had gone far
a ghost appeared from the shadows

With a measure of revenge to exact
I could never have known

And before I could defend ourselves
and assess our lot

The villain had hit his mark
as a shot rang on the dock

I turned and cradled her whom I'd just met
She closed her beautiful blue eyes

And left me alone again yet again
as I bowed my head and cried

In that moment I was for a moment bitter
Giving up my muffled cries

Pray you never hold a beautiful woman
as she leaves you and dies

A Burning House

Lord, reach down to my shingles

and tell me are they warm to Your touch

Where, oh where are the people who once swore to us

That they care so much

My stucco bubbles and cracks with the heat

That's tearing down my walls

Is there no one anywhere

Who cares less at all

No fire burns in the hearth

There is no need for more

For all the fire needed

is burning on my floor

In my bedrooms once quite warm

where sweet love was once raised

Passion never knew the intensity

now that they are ablaze

Out in my garden tropic

where cool Pacific winds did cool

Are all the stock in a Shakespearean play

Only now it is the tableau fool

For I am a burning house

not alone in this inferno

As if as Joan my stake burns

Though I do not burn alone

Come please reclamation

and make me beautiful then

But please allow me hidden

Until I see you again

WREATH OF TEARS

Some days go quite well

and you live life full no matter if until

You know your glass will always be full

No matter what you spill

Abandon I imagine is

something akin to flying

There's nothing but space above you

And the solid ground waits

you always come to

Perhaps as if but on two wheels

with a wind you create

coursing through your hair

And by the time you brush it away

You find again it's there

But the fun is as if in a plane

And you shut the engine down

as you plummet to the earth

You don't hear a sound

Unlike when you roll those two wheels

you tumble and you taste the dirt

You get up, dust yourself laughing, saying

"Hey, I've been through worse"

That my friend is living

When fear is all that dies

When it's only the joyous ones looking on

are the only ones who cry

That's the only way to do it

to do mark the time in years

And if in fact you do so you leave a legacy

And never a wreath of tears

My Fountain

Have you ever stared into a fountain

The water trips and falls

it splashes and dances

But goes nowhere at all

Yet it never ceases to fascinate

Though it does the same cartwheels over and over

Tapping its own surface like

the podium of a composer

And in the sunlight through its spray

If you look closely so

You'll swear you can there

See a lovely rainbow

And the stream as it parts

Seems like crystals tumbling through

And make no mistake

they are fashioned only for you

So go ahead and gaze away

And see anything you like

but no matter how you try

You'll see anything but the night

You are in fact my fountain

and everything we do is different everyday

It's how the water rises and splashes down

Is only yours and none other's way

KEEPER

Where is my weary heart

please where has it gone

Does it float on a breeze

Captured in some love song

I spent some time in places

Where I ought not have been

Carousing with women whom with

I should never have been

I was in love once

Such a long, long time ago

But it a time of weakness

I simply let her go

I took a train up to Memphis

And on then to Chicago

To let my music take me

As far as I might go

But finding no peace

No answer to my dreams

I headed back home

to my old New Orleans

I grazed the lurid streets

And thought of sowing wild seeds

I thought that I may so

To satisfy my needs

But when invited to do so

By a sultry siren

I simply told her no

And I took my leave then

So I set about once again

in my tired old search

To find whom I'd left cruelly

alone in the lurch

One midnight I saw beneath

a dimly lit streetlight

Through a foggy heavy evening

I saw in the light

There was no mistake

And I knew I was right

Stepping from the shadows

A figure came into the light

Gathering myself up

I knew what I must do

That night I again found my heart

Whose keeper had been you

THE SUMMER OF '72

There's an old dirt road that I know

that runs along a verdant field

Sometimes I part the barbed wire and run through

Just to remember how it feels

I ran there when I was a boy

on my way to Crystal Creek

Pretending when once I would there find

the lovely love whom I did seek

But time and again it was but I

who did go for a swim alone

Up until dinnertime when

my mother would call me home

One summer Saturday though

things were different

There was a certain music in the air

And almost as if by magic I looked up

And saw you bathing there

I asked if I might join you

and as if you had had this all in mind

You motioned to me as if on cue

In a softly way so kind

We passed the afternoon

As two young lovers often do

I suppose by then my mother may have called

But all I could hear was you

We go back now to Crystal Creek

now with a grandchild or two

Only because we shared a swim that day

I the summer of '72

FOLLOW ME

Tell me, father, where does one go

when the world becomes so wretched and cruel

That man turns against man

Having drunk from hatred's pool

Why are some souls forgotten

and for some perverse need

Call out for recognition

through some deadly malicious deed

Are we not all God's children

were we not all born of the same bed

Why have some taken up the sword

while others rested their heads

Is there, father, a place

where peace can ever be

Yes, my son, and I know of the place

You need but follow me

Without A Voice

I sought not to be a writer

and yet I scribe these lines

Nor thought to be a musician

And though here I am keeping time

I thought perhaps a builder

of beautiful buildings just so

Where people may like to live

or at least at times to come and go

As things sometimes do

I built a modest place where people would come and exchange
what they thought

And found what they found there

Was more than they had brought

Once it was anchored

And its beams stood tall and strong

When done I never once visited it

I just left it there along

Sometime later an important man called me

And said you must come and visit

just what has come to be

I reluctantly agreed to go there

To find what could possibly be

He met me when I arrived

He said keep your ears open

and your eyes peeled

And once inside let me please know just what it is you feel

I heard a familiar chorus I had written

To certain poet's prose inscribed saying as I once did

Without a voice a poem will never be a song

Kind Of Comfort

Midnight in New Orleans

down by the river on the docks

Throwing stones into the water thinking

what I have and what I've not

I've got a house back up in the Northshore wood

You wouldn't ever know you found it

even if you ever could

I've got some acres there

that are just across my creek

I find refuge there sometimes

when I find myself weak

I've a gun hanging o'er my fireplace I use mostly

To keep the raccoons that come by at bay

But on occasion I use it

to fetch dinner for the day

Lost in my thoughts I didn't realize

a woman had approached from behind

As I gazed into the Mississippi

speaking so ever kind

She said "You look kind of lonely Sugar

Is there something I can do"

I said "Oh, thank you ma'am, but no

I'm afraid I'd not be worthy of you"

She replied "Oh come on honey,

what say we just go for a drink"

Shyly I said "Well, if it'll be alright

if that's what you think"

So, we went up to Decatur

and then on to Esplanade

All the while hoping this wouldn't turn out to be

some mistake that I had made

But the evening went quite nicely

more so that I thought would be

She offered the kind of comfort

it had been so long for me to see

As I went to pay the bill

seems she slipped into the night

And though alone

a feeling fell upon me saying

Everything would be alright

THE MANSION OF LONG COLUMNS

It's down along the shaded lane

known as Esplanade Avenue

The oaks have protected her

for one hundred year and two

There are beautiful houses

flanking her ample shoulders

You could try and find her where

her fire shows to smoulder

She has witnessed wars

and such loss of life and limb

Such as one would never ask

such her story to begin

There upon her grounds do bloom

yellow roses and daffodils

Which will bloom so faithfully

 as August comes until

Where you ask is this place I mention

and can it be ever found

Why yes, my son, but do lean in

for escape from us no sound

You will never find what you seek

if you but simply follow them

Instead, the grand dame stately rests

The mansion of long columns

At Home Anymore

I went knocking one afternoon

on my good friend's front door

And I found something there

that I'd not seen before

I rang the bell there waiting

and I called out his name

But the quiet I first met there

During there did still remain

Again, I called out to the yard

with no response returned

Only finally to come and realize

I was alone I learned

I drove across town to visit

another long well-known friend

Only to have my journey

as before meet a likewise end

Where has everyone gone

where have they gone to

And why not did they call to ask

if I'd like to go too

Why must people go other places

where things are unknown and strange

Why does a roving spirit constantly

Always pine for a change

Can you please tell me kindly

why such friends thirst for more

Tell me if you can, does no one

stay at home anymore

Do Not Cry For New Orleans

The evening was supposed to welcome

A New Year to begin

With celebratory bells swaying

For one and all hear ring

But rather in the dead of night

Evil stalked happiness to rout

To wreak havoc the kind of which

For some time be talked about

But let us please remember

This is New Orleans after all

Where people come to see and do

That which they may not recall

And upon this savage act

Perpetrated on the innocent

People will give quarter not

This pathetic malcontent

Soon there will be second lines

Parading down the avenue

As for you who burns now

No one will remember you

And to all who know her

The rouged lady that she fairs

She invites you back to see her

And she waits to welcome you there

And she sends a message

For those who will hold tight the dream

Come and see me please

And do not cry for New Orleans

Pained Queen Of New Orleans

It was the dawning of a New Year

and of a new day

With beautiful winter skies greeting

as such you couldn't say

But just then evil rang out

upon the Bourbon Street Fifteen

The likes of which through storms and floods

not even Essex had never seen

A disillusioned madman attacked

taking all found in his way

Where or why this veteran did so

and when did he go astray

Did we abandon him

he who once protected us

Was there something more we could have done

And if so, what would be such

Rest you heavy shoulders

down where what's not what it seems

And return you once again

Please pained queen of New Orleans

New Orleans Call

Things are rarely all they seem

'Specially if you find yourself Walking the shady streets

down in old New Orleans

A mime on a street corner

seems locked in a box unseen

Shielding cake makeup eyes

from scant clouded sunbeams

A dancer in a window

offers a sultry fetching glow

Letting you know there's more to the dance

That a young man may ever know

A policeman munches a Lucky Dog

outside the Royal Orleans

While upstairs is a man reliving

what were forgotten dreams

Jazz flows from fine clubs

from musicians made everyday

And if ask you what that just might be

Well I simply cannot say

Down the street flows the river

the Mississippi calls your name

And though you try to answer you find

Your still may go insane

But that's what brought you here

to forget where you came from

To sit in Jackson Square and hear

St. Louis Cathedral's bells when rung

So, come you to New Orleans

and have your eyes betrayed

And I dare you try and fight New Orleans call

begging you to stay

From my chilly balcony I see

lights strung down the street

And I listen intently that I may hear

The snow landing on concrete

But no sound like my own voice

it seems is yet heard

All that echoes it appears to consider

The day's lessons learned

Was today I a good man

or did I disappoint

Was I given absolution and

will Farther John come and anoint

Did I call my mother

and did she answer me

I'm sure she did but please know she I can no longer see

And across the room next to my fire

Sitting beneath all my art and books

A woman I cannot figure she could f me

Would simply usually overlook

Garnet hued embers smolder

where burning timbers tumble

Such that looking in her emerald eyes

This Year True

Twenty years ago, this evening

was an evening of gowns and tails

As we headed out into the night

To see what would prevail

There would be fine food and music

And flow would the champagne

Until nothing more than memories

Would be all that would remain

Overhead fireworks explode

to trumpet times a coming

Such that we've not witnessed

They would bring

Oh, all the colors flashing

lighting up a glorious night

And to the east I know I see

a new dawning light

Gather us all in the town square

and amid the New Year bells peeling

Be glad we each are there

So to you all in the coming time

may your dreams rest with you

And all that you deserve

visit this year true

MILE NINE

It's my tour to put in the next two weeks

Down here in Pilot town

Where it's up to me to make sure no ships find

A sand bar and run aground

Down here where the marsh gives way

To the delta river's mouth

It's lonely to be sure down here

Taking the big boats further south

They're going places I've been to

And no longer care to go

I've been most places that draw their water

from the Gulf of Mexico

Not a bad life really and the money's always good

Doesn't matter anyway 'cos down here

There's nowhere to spend it

if you could

I just got a radio call saying

You wait at Mile Marker 10

Checking my maps I see

That it's just around the next bend

I approach the 9th

And coming up on me there

Is a ship no one has tracked

and down on me she does stare

There was no time to veer

somehow out of her path

It seemed soon I would be held in

the Mississippi's grasp

I'll not make past Mile 9

Nor shall I see Mile 10

But in my maritime dreams

I will see you again

Take It Down

When at times it seems as though

your world's not turning 'round

Pause a moment and then you'll hear

The joy found in the absence of sound

When it seems your shoulders

feel so weighted down

Stop and take a rest my friend

'til your strength can be found

If you feel as though you've lost your way

and fear's trepidation is a hound

Buckle up your courage in your enemy's face

And quietly stare him down

If at times it seems you're overwhelmed

And your insecurity has stood its ground

Meet it face to face and in one fell swoop

Laugh and take it down

Nashville Dreams

Boarded a train out in L. A.

'Cos nothing there's what it seems

On my way there find it out where it's at

Going down to New Orleans

They've got whiskey flowing there all night

And lovely ladies there waiting too

If you're lucky like I once was friend

To might find both of them for

you too

I left one I so loved so long ago

Going to find if anyone knows of her

And where it is she'd go

One gentleman remembered her

But was sad to tell me still

Seems she took a fast airplane

To go up there to Nashville

He told me she once mentioned me

And was heartbroken when I split

And that she apparently didn't make your plan

And that that was about it

He further said she'd gone to do it

To finally chase her dreams

And in a deserved turnabout play

You didn't fit hers it seems

Lyrics Find Their Melody

I sit alone with the wood

While you call it a night

Up to bed leaving me wondering

If I treated you quite alright

I search and try to find

The proper and lasting lyric

And when you offer your melody

I know I've found the music

You comfort in the darkness

As your light shows me the way

And when I find I'm lost for words

You let me know that it's okay

And when I leave the house

Not knowing where to go

Your song carries me along

As if the way is one you know

And so that's how a song's composed

And how that it should be

When the lights dim as I am on the stage

My lyrics find their melody

THE COMPOSER

I was trying to learn a song

It wasn't the chords I found hard

Just the lesson escaping

I couldn't quite record

The lyrics are always lurking

Present in my head

Why I always find it difficult

Because they follow me to bed

The composer is conflicted

Finding things hard to understand

He's one you would know

For I am that man

THE CHRISTMAS NOON

It seems there are some presents resting

Beneath our Christmas tree

Only one or two for you

And the rest for me

What I have done to deserve such

I think you know I love you

But don't you know quite enough

how I do so much do

But let us now to celebrate

Christmas has come none too soon

And shall we feast with family

Well past the Christmas noon

ROSES

I'm going to the moon

And on my way to Ptolemy

To capture a star or two

But for you and none for me

When I one day do return

I will build you a castle

It will be of stone and turrets

And a fire there will cackle

I'll will then construct a carriage

Of gold and lavender

To ride in which will be

What you will always remember

And when you return

The road to our home will be

Tossed with roses

By those whom hide in the woods

Their names no one ever knows

Our Glass

On a desk upon a cold midnight

A single candle nestled burns

Where at times were not kind

Hard lessons were sometimes learned

But here we are at Christmastime

Let us be ever thankful

For what we all have true

And that our glass is ever full

GARDEN OF THE HEART

Could I ever pen a piece

That would make women pause and cry

That would make strong men question themselves why

There is such a place

That only few do know

It's where dreams are wrought

And the future seeds are sown

Where, oh where you wonder

Could there a place where sighs are far apart

Why, my son easily enough known

It is the garden of the heart

THIS SEASON

I wish I were a great man

but perhaps a good one no less

To give you all that I have

and it being my best

During this lovely season

with Christmas on the call

May we all be thankful

for what we have one and all to all this season when

We have such to be thankful for

Let us be reminded of we had before

His Star

She sleeps soundly throughout the night

And such is she what one should do

While restless, I sit up and write

With words I'm given to

It's three in the morning

And I write what I cannot say

The kind of thoughts always best heard

On another day

But I wish you rest my love

For you no doubt has travelled far

Just like please keep looking overhead

And remain under His star

Unaware

Will I be a wave that crashes

only once upon the shore

Or will I be followed

by ones which have not come before

Will I be a thought

that soon may be forgotten

Or a man who leaves some thought kindly begotten

Will I make a difference

in someone else's life

Who may find themselves foundering in a lost strife

There is an answer

to be found somewhere

Let me know if you find

that which I am unaware

An Unwritten Play

When I get to the summit

Of the mountain's peak

Will I then if ever

Find what it is I seek

Or should I be a miner

In search of buried gold

Would that be the riches

I could finally hold

Or should I be a playwright

And spin mysteries of the heart

If I were could you

Perhaps play the lead part

It's a wide world to be sure

And many kinds to make one's way

Can you be a player

In an unwritten play

Bow and Strings

Rosin up the bow and strings

Polish the piano and violins

And gather up the children's choir

That we may hear them sing

Christmas carols in the snow

All the ones that you well know

Wrap yourself well

To keep you ever warm so

Christmas visits us quite sweetly

One to make memories

We will hold so deeply

So a Merry Christmas

To you one and all

And a bit of warm cider

As we deck the halls

DECLARATION

IRISH CREED

We don't count

We don't wear watches

We're rolling!

www.ingramcontent.com/pod-product-compliance
Lightning Source LLC
Chambersburg PA
CBHW06091525O626
47159CB00008B/3017